YO
OUT

WILLIAM DENNING

Series editor Jeanne Hinton

HUNT&
THORPE

Copyright © 1992 Hunt & Thorpe
Text © 1992 by William Denning
Illustrations © 1992 by Len Munnik
Originally published by Hunt & Thorpe 1992

ISBN 1 85608 185 0

In Australia this book is published by:
Hunt & Thorpe Australia Pty Ltd.
9 Euston Street, Rydalmere NSW 2116

A CIP catalogue record for this book is available from
the British Library

Manufactured in the United Kingdom

CONTENTS

■ INTRODUCTION

In the beginning God created the heavens and
the earth.
The earth was without form and void
and darkness was upon the face of the deep;
and the Spirit of God was moving over the
face of the waters …
… Then God said 'Let us make humankind in
our image …' (RSV)

That is another way of saying that creativity is
built into us from the beginning; it is our right
and joy, and God delights in all our making and
doing, renewing and discovering. There is
immeasurable pleasure for God in the whole
range of our creating from music and poetry to
food, flowers and decorating, and from paint
and clay to banners, collage and calligraphy, to
say nothing of wood carving, basket making and
the rest.

When we get down to it and get lost in the
fascination of it, amazing and exciting things
happen, yet in fact we often seem to insist that

we are not creative or artistic, and that we cannot do anything creative. We are caught between a deep desire to be imaginatively creative and a conviction or fear that it is impossible. In this booklet we shall look at what some of those blocks to our essential creativity might be. While obviously, not everyone can do everything, there could be an area that fires your enthusiasm and it might be rather like a hidden path in a wood that calls you on though you cannot even begin to know what is waiting there in the mysterious depths.

Somewhere in you below the surface, there are springs of artistic creativity longing to be set free and you may well not have the remotest idea what they might be. A caterpillar quietly chewing a leaf and vaguely aware of the delicate creature fluttering above its head, does not know that one day it will be like that butterfly; if it could speak, it would insist that such a thing would not be possible. Beware of saying too soon that you cannot make or do something that is truly beautiful; your hands and your imagination await their moment.

If you can get in touch with that artistic

creative self, some very good things will certainly happen. For a start you will be healthier and more satisfied. You will be a more interesting person to have around and a more knowledgable one. Skills will be developed that can save money and it may well be possible to make and do things for your own interest and for the home that at first seemed totally out of the question.

There can be such enormous satisfaction in the struggle and achievement of being creative. It is not just a device for handling stress, avoiding boredom or saving money, though those may be incentives; it is much more about being your own true self, the self that no one yet knows. It will mean going on a new journey of discovery and God will share it with you. Do take the risk and silence those negative voices that say you are no good. Those voices have got it wrong.

Creativity at its best is about God's work in and through us, going on doing what God wants to do with the universe and thoroughly enjoying seeing it happen. Creation is still happening and we have the option of being part of the exciting process or of being demoralised spectators.

It might be worth asking where the yearning to liberate your artistic self has come from. For some reason a deep urge has stirred in your depths. Perhaps there is a lot of stress around and there is a need to find good ways of relaxing. Possibly for the first time in years there is time or opportunity to do what you could only dream about before. Maybe the children have gone at last (though they will be back) or redundancy has struck. Maybe the half feared, half longed for retirement has finally come. That deep hunger may have surfaced as part of your spiritual journey as suddenly you saw that prayer could be much more than spoken words. That frequently happens in Creativity Workshops where over the years I have seen countless numbers of people surprised, amazed and excited at the discovery of an unrecognised ability with colour, words, movement or music, and they have seen its link with worship. Before the workshop, most would have said quite firmly that they would not be able to do it.

The journey from those early stirrings of

excited interest to a deep level of fulfilment, need not be as hard as we might at first imagine.

There will always be struggle, but that struggle is not without its pleasures and satisfactions.

The EXERCISES that are included need to be given time and space; do not rush them and do make notes to keep for reference; the very act of writing is itself valuable; an added dimension is to find a good friend who will let you talk through the exercise afterwards, listening and encouraging you and certainly not criticising what you say.

■ EXERCISE 1

The AIM is to recall childhood memories of being creative and to learn from what was good or bad about those experiences.

Recall your earliest memories of making or doing something creative. What feelings belong to that time? Were they enjoyable or painful, frustrating or satisfying?

Recall your earliest experiences of wonder and awe. Was there beauty, mystery, sadness, joy or anything else. What sort of situations produced these times?

In your present life, how many of these feelings do you experience, and which ones do you want to enlarge and enjoy? Remember, the choice is your's.

■ 1

BLOCKS AND BARRIERS

EVERY DAY WITHOUT ever thinking about it, we are artists of a kind. This is expressed in what we do with colours and fabrics in our homes and with our choice of clothes. We do it with flowers indoors and with gardens outdoors. Even while day-dreaming, we are writing stories that probably will never see the light of day, but they are stories, and often highly imaginative ones at that. The preparation and presentation of food is an art in its own right even though there may not be the time to do it with the care we prefer.

Why is it that we have such doubts about our creativity if we are already doing things with thoughtfulness, imagination and considerable skill? And how can we get past the dark and destructive negativity that prevents us from making things that are good and beautiful?

Self-doubt is one of the most imprisoning of qualities and one of the hardest to leave behind.

It seems that we take self-doubt into our system from our earliest days and will not or cannot challenge its power. This may have come from the persistent critical attitude of parents or parental figures in infancy, though they probably thought they were encouraging or disciplining. It might have been the disapproval of a teacher at school or the teasing by other children that wrecked self-confidence. I am sure that criticism by parents and teachers is well-intentioned but it can be experienced as something quite devastating. Regularly in workshops people tell us how their treachers laughed at what they did or tore up their paintings. I am not so sure that they really did do quite such awful things but it clearly felt like it and the experience remains as something quite crippling in adult life.

Competition can be another deadly force, though obviously for some it is a powerful stimulus to achievement. Both the pressure to compete with others and the need to be successful may be fine for the few who make it in their chosen spheres, but there are many more who will never make it on those terms. We live in a society that is committed to

achieving in terms of money, power and success. We need money of course, and we have to live in some sort of structure, and we do not want sloppy inadequate standards, but does that have to mean an abrasively competitive culture where those perceived to be poor, weak and incompetent have no value? They are overflowing with unacknowledged gifts. Those who are in prison are released, the lame walk, the deaf hear and the blind see.

Letting your artist go free is precisely about this kind of enpowerment. It could be about getting out of limiting prisons of fear and self-doubt, and that deeply destructive sense of not being able to do anything really well. It is about finding the freedom to walk with God into unknown places with courage and faith instead of hobbling along feeling left behind. There is a new entering into life instead of feeling deaf and blind, cut off and out of touch with others and with the remarkably rich and beautiful universe. Artists learn to walk in a way that takes risks with their eyes and ears wide open and alert to miss nothing.

The capacity to play without inhibition or

self-conciousness is another key element in this exploration of what blocks our movement. There is little doubt that we largely associate play with children and we keep it firmly there.

There is a message in this about adult life being too serious for children's games. And yet we know very well in our hearts that Jesus was absolutely right when he reminded us that unless we become as little children, the good things in life are closed off from us.

Children at their best play with imagination and spontaneity, and have no fear of pastels on paper or being in the percussion band at All Age Worship. They press anybody and everything into use when absorbed in a game that needs props, and adults are drawn into the play too. Their love of stories is phenomenal and my oldest grandson frequently asks me to tell him about when I was a little boy. He is on to a winner because we both love to hear about the days that have gone.

There is a lovely translation of Proverbs 8 in the Jerusalem Bible where the writer is speaking of Wisdom as creator at the beginning of time, who is at God's side 'ever at play' and 'at play everywhere in the world', delighting God and delighting to be with people. Sadly, children sometimes stop, or are stopped from, playing and cease delighting, and the gift of play is lost.

Words like artist, poet, actor, musician, sculptor or dancer can cause some hang-ups also as they are somehow linked with special gifts and special people who are not like the rest of us. While it is perfectly clear that some people have obvious gifts that others of us do not have, it is simply not true to put such people in a different world. The gospel reminds us that we are all full of limitless possibility if we can get past the blocks and barriers that sit so heavily just beneath the level of our consciousness. We need to challenge the corrupting assumptions behind those blocks and barriers for the only power they have is what we allow them to have, and with God's help, that power can go for ever.

Finally, let us look again at the powerful and dynamic picture at the beginning of the Bible. There we have the brooding Spirit of God hovering over the chaos waiting, always waiting, to set creation free and to bring order, growth and change. For humanity, change is threatening, and therefore, there is an enormous investment in not changing. But, if in your heart, the artist has stirred, then for your sake and God's sake, listen to that stirring. The Spirit of God is brooding over your depths.

■ EXERCISE 2

The AIM is to explore experiences of approval in the past and in the present, and to check out their significance.

• Recall an early memory from school days of disapproval. What did it make you feel about yourself and what you were doing?

• Recall a memory of approval from the same setting, and see how that felt. Maybe you cannot remember it ever happening; how does that feel?

• Think back over the past few weeks; can you recall something creative that you have made, said or done that was useful, beautiful, enjoyable and felt good. Was it met by approval or disapproval or perhaps worse still, was it not even noticed?

• The responses of other people are terribly

important to us; can you challenge the power of early or recent disapprovals, and will you choose to focus on the affirming approving voices? Do talk to that friend you trust about these things.

■ 2

A STIRRING IN THE DEPTHS

RESPONDING TO THIS inner prompting from God to liberate the imaginative, child–like self, is much more than having a pleasant hobby to wile away the dark winter evenings, or for having fun on holiday; it will be all that, but so very much more. It is about a way of life that can grow and grow beyond all expectations and in directions of which we are not yet aware. It is a spiritual journey, and it is about taking that path deep into the unknown woods.

Another image would be that we lift our eyes to the distant horizon where we glimpse the splendid mystery of the Holy One and we journey towards that mystery only to find that God has never been anywhere but by our side. Art in its many forms helps us touch the edge of mystical experience and to find some real expression of it.

Not only is it the beyondness and the wonder

of God that are perceived; it is desperately important for our own growth that we are in touch with what we feel within ourselves. In that sense it is also a healing journey that is made possible by our liberated creativity. It is not so much about gift as about having the courage and desire to get past the inhibitions, fears and prejudices deep inside. They clutter us unbearably and have grown over many years and will not go away overnight. We dare not ignore those deep feelings that are way below the surface; they can emerge at the most unlikely times and cause havoc.

Time spent with raw materials, imagination and an open mind can be enormously therapeutic, whether it is an attempt to respond to the infinite wonder and beauty of the world around or whether it is expressing deep inner feelings. At the start, we are unlikely to be able to produce excellent likenesses of that beauty, or adequate expressions of those feelings, so let us put aside ideas of having to do well for the time being. It is sufficient to do what we can. Let us again recall how a little girl behaves when absorbed in her playfulness with wax crayons;

ordinarily she will not be hunted by the pursuit of excellence and it is enough that she loves the colours on the paper as they are. The little boy helping with the pastry does not seem unduly worried by the soil from the garden that has joined his little pastry figures; to him they are beautiful because he has made them. The joy and the wholeness are in the doing, not in the technical perfection of the result. That is one of the big distinctions between being a professional and what we are thinking about here. Skill comes later with appropriate training and hard work, but the starting point involves letting go of trying to be perfect on day one. Such and attitude is an invitation to frustration and despair.

If it is true that within us there is a playful yearning child, it is also true that there is often an angry, disapproving parent who repeatedly reminds us that we are not good enough; though that same parent voice can be nurturing and kindly it is not so frequently heard. One disapproving word needs scores of approving ones to make up the loss and heal the wounds. But we do have the power to choose and that is the adult way. We can choose to let go of what is destructive and focus on the enabling, affirming, liberating things – like being fully in the moment, deeply aware of the beauty around and in people, and truly seeing what is there, however unsatisfactory our attempts at portrayal.

The brooding, stirring Spirit of God calls us first to see and to be aware and to walk with awe through the world. It is more important that we wait in stillness and see with reverence, than get stressed and tense about trying to be perfect.

■ EXERCISE 3

The AIM is to see more clearly and more deeply.

• Walk around your house and find an object or look out of the window and focus on something familiar; note its colour, texture and shape; is it beautiful or ugly and do you like or dislike it? What does it make you feel? Are you comfortable or uncomfortable with it? What about its setting and how it relates to its environment? If it is possible, touch and feel it.

• When you really begin to SEE that object

with deep awareness, unique in its setting with today's light, colour and everything else, you are doing something reverent and important, because all things matter to God.

• Write down a few thoughts about your seeing exercise; what did you see in the familiar that you had not seen before and what did you feel?

• Artists learn to SEE. Sometimes on holiday I specially want to sketch but it simply will not happen to my satisfaction. I then comfort myself with a deep truth; even if the drawing is unsatisfactory. I have looked carefully and slowly and have seen. To see with deep awareness is the opposite of an apathetic blindness that survives in a dull monotonous world without a soul.

All of this has little or nothing to do with competence or skill, but it has everything to do with a spiritual approach to creativity; competence will come in time with encouragement and practice.

■ 3

CREATIVITY, SPIRITUALITY AND LIFESTYLE

I N OUR COMPLEX and beautiful yet wounded world, everything is interwoven and God is intimately involved in this cosmic tapestry at every point and beyond. Therefore we are not able to talk about spirituality as if it were a separate subject like nuclear physics or organic gardening. It would be as senseless as trying to talk about being in love without referring to people and relationships. Because I am fortunate enough to live in an old farmhouse in the heart of the countryside, people who come here sometimes say how lovely it must be to live 'away from it all.' The truth is that we can never get away from life, and somehow we have to learn how to live with balance and integrity in a world where there is fear, greed and hatred. And where there seems often to be a wanton destruction of beauty in the interests of personal wealth and power. It is part of our self-deception to think that we are not in all of this, and that if only we could get away or escape from it to a brave and wonderful new world, life could be whole and good.

So our human dilemma is a double bind. At one level we think we are 'no good' and will not believe in our amazing possibilities, largely because of our childhood experiences. At another level, when we see how awful people can be to one another, we are sure that we would not do things like that. We are blind to our potential to do things that are good and beautiful, and to our capacity to be limitlessly destructive. The same hands that do indescribably delicate surgery can kill another person with jealous hatred. The same mind that can conceive technologies that save lives can conceive weapons of mass destruction.

It is our joy and delight and it is our awesome responsibility to ensure that human creativity is fully integrated with the spiritual journey, and that there is no separation from daily lifestyle. It is as true at a corporate level as it is at a private and personal one.

Creativity, therefore, is not an escape from reality, nor a diversion from harsh circumstances. It is true that we all need solitude from time to time and we need space to breathe when the pressure is on, but I have to say that setting your artist free offers more than the promise of pleasant little interludes in a busy schedule. It will do some of that, but it will do so much more than that, and it is the 'more than that' that is the cutting edge that has bite and meaning. This is the point where struggle and ecstasy are found.

Love again, is the analogy. Human love promises far more than pleasant little interludes in a busy life – it offers pain as well as delight, and struggle as well as harmony, if there is to be growth in that loving relationship. It means meeting and facing the unpalatable truths of the loved one, as well as the acceptable and attractive side. And it means acknowledging the truth of one's own shadowed humanity.

Whatever sort of artist you might want to be, sooner or later the challenge will be there to move beyond the surface and to enter more fully into the reality of the earth, its inhabitants and the cosmos. This means exploring the light and the dark, the glory and the shadow, all the time looking for truth and beauty, determined to believe in the essential goodness of what God is making and doing. It is to begin to join the divine acclamation of Genesis 1, when after each dramatic unfolding, God saw that 'it was good'. It is early in the same story that the dark shadow crosses the idyllic picture, and so also must we face the harsh truth of a wounded creation. Creativity does not offer an escape route from reality; it offers a way of exploring and integrating our understanding of the mystery of God's love in a world that is both wounded yet magnificent.

The gospel we believe includes hope and promise. The liberated artist holds that belief and wants to share with other people a sense of awe and wonder as creation reveals her treasures to those who have eyes to see. And artists disguised as architects, planners, designers, and builders can make life more beautiful. It matters that people are surrounded by the beauty of trees rather than the squalor of broken glass and the ugliness of urban decay or the boredom of dull and meaningless design. The poetry of the Psalms revels in the magnificence of what is around us – frightening even in that magnificence. Those same Psalms do not hesitate to point out terrifying consequences when humanity acts against the interests of one another, and of creation of which we are an integral part. Ugliness is against the will of God and God desires that the creative gifts in humanity be used to enrich the quality of life for all, whether in a country village or in a vast urban building development.

Another aspect of the linking of creativity and spirituality is prayer. Praying for some may be natural and easy, but for others of us that is not so. Practical expressions of creativity can be full of possibility for our devotional life, which is more about contemplation and meditation than about words which can get in the way. Some spiritual traditions make prayer almost exclusively a verbal process, and from us towards God at that! There are at least two levels at which this non-verbal praying may occur. One is where the absorption with what is happening is so complete that without ever saying so, the person is intimately involved with God; it is unconscious prayer. The other level is where there is a deliberate and conscious attempt to use an art form to express visually what is felt deeply in order to offer that expression to God. Futhermore there is a combination of both where the one creating is so moved with awe and wonder that the act becomes a silent meditative prayer that 'sees God in all things and all things in God' to quote Mechtild of Magdeburg writing in the 13th century.

Reverence for Creator and creation, which

the pursuit of art involves, inevitably means a
commitment to a green way of life and,
consequently, a radically changing lifestyle. This
sharing with God in the joy and anguish of
creating, has a price. No longer can we go
round with our eyes closed to the ravaging of
natural resources and the uncaring abuse and
exploitation of the poor. Again and again artists,
whether professional or amateur, have pointed
out injustice and oppression in society. Both
beauty and ugliness are the focus of their
attentiveness and communication. Creativity,
spirituality and lifestyle are so interwoven as to

be inseparable. Being creatively artistic, loving God and attentively caring for humanity, the earth and all its creatures belong together. It is one huge, costly and infinitely rewarding process.

In a word, creativity opens your eyes. Like Pandora's Box, once opened, there is no going back.

■ EXERCISE 4

The AIM is to see with imaginative creativity, and to take that experience into private prayer.

• Go outside and look for a leaf that interests you to take home; note its texture, shape, colours and structure.

• Now put it to one side and draw it as carefully as you can remember it; do not be too hard on yourself if the drawing is not as good as you might like.

• If you have paints or pastels, look at your leaf and see if you can get some of those colours it has, or might have in other seasons. You might care to make a pattern with those colours, using the shape of the leaf as an inspiration.

• Now close your eyes and use imagination to

see and feel the leaf emerging from its bud warmed by the spring sunshine. Follow it on through the seasons until it finally falls gently to the earth at the end of its days. Focus on its interesting beauty and on its flaws and wounds and note how it feels.

• Make a note of those images and feelings which you most readily identify with. Feel and think about them.

• Finally, take the leaf in your hands as a symbol of your own life and hold those feelings, one by one, in the loving accepting presence of God.

■ 4

GETTING IT RIGHT

IT WILL BE helpful at this point to take a brief look at how we process information. Some relevant and interesting research on how the brain works has been commented on by Betty Edwards in her book *Drawing on the Right Side of the Brain*. She relies heavily on research done at the California Institute of Technology in the fifties and sixties. It is from these studies, which involved patients who had experienced brain surgery, that the conclusion was reached that the two halves of the brain work in different but complementary ways.

Without going into technical details it is perfectly possible to accept the reasonable assumption that some people use one half more than the other. The left side of the brain is more rational and analytical and uses words; it is very controlling and has everything in its place. The right side is more intuitive and sensitively responsive, being rather dreamy yet creative. In some ways it is the paradox of order and chaos.

When it comes to drawing and creativity, it is the right side we need to use most. This is as much as anything a mood or attitude. I often have problems getting started with painting or sketching. An impatient, organising left-brain voice orders me to get on and get it done quickly. "Just a quick sketch", it says, "before moving on." But the right-brain artist voice invites me to slow down and take it gently and quietly, to give time to look around and see in depth. When that destructive voice finally accepts that I am going to take time and not hurry, it tries another approach. "Keep to something familiar that you know you can do", and so it goes on urging me to play safe and to keep to familiar subjects that can be drawn almost from habit. The left brain has everything in compartments, with its standard beech tree, its standard bit of wall, and grasses all carefully recorded to push on to the paper instead of actually drawing this particular tree, and that specially unique bit of wall with grass that has no other grass quite like it.

Then when I attempt something I know I cannot draw, the tempting voices suggest many ways out of the threatening failure. Somehow, we have to break with those initial responses and controlling, demoralising voices. If we listen to them, we stay locked up for ever. Once we break free, taking the risk that we might actually be able to do the very thing we thought we could not, a new dimension is upon us.

■ EXERCISE 5

The AIM is to draw in a way that will help to get the right side of the brain working. It sounds odd, but the idea is to copy a drawing that is upside down. It needs to be a line drawing like a cartoon – in fact a cartoon from the paper would be ideal. So in addition to that you need your pencil and paper and do avoid looking at the picture before you begin.

• When you are ready, turn the drawing round so that the top is at the bottom, and then copy it line by line as carefully as you can.

• When you have finished I think you will find that your copy looks rather better than you expected, and much better than if you had tried to do it the right way up. There is a simple explanation: had you tried to copy the drawing the right way up, you would have attempted to draw what you already thought each part should look like because you already knew what it was (left brain). Because you were unable to recognise the upside down shapes you could only draw what you could see (right brain). We learn to see what is there and not what we think ought to be there.

5

TAKING THE PLUNGE

YOU HAVE BEGUN to explore your creativity in some of the simple exercises already given. Where would you like to go next? The following sections suggest the possibility of a number of different art forms. Be aware as you read through them which ideas catch your imagination or stir your longing. You might even want to stop and try your hand at one or another of the options en route before you go any further. It could be with paint trying to portray some landscape that fascinates you, or attempting to carve a piece of driftwood, or it might be writing poetry, or making a collage with scrap materials. It might well be worth trying a wide range of different possibilities, so do experiment and do not be put off by apparent failures.

If the inclination is towards painting, then it is worth avoiding cheap paper and brushes; watercolour, acrylics, pastels and charcoal are all relatively inexpensive as part of the initial finding out process. As time goes on and it becomes more clear where your interest and ability are taking you, it might well be appropriate to join a group developing that skill or to buy some helpful books in the area of your choice.

Arts and crafts are often put together for exhibition purposes but there are significant differences between them, though they are both very much about creativity; an understanding of those differences might prove helpful in making choices.

Making a beautiful tapestry from a prepared plan is very different from sitting outside sketching an unfamiliar group of cottages that has caught your eye. Crafts rely more on learned skills and there is usually an element of repetition working to a pre-determined plan possibly prepared by someone else. That could be true of a stool made to a design for instance. providing the plan is followed carefully, the result is totally predictable. Many years ago I made a small sailing dinghy from prepared drawings; it was an enormous pleasure to play with marine ply and glue, using tools to shape the wood, finally painting and varnishing the whole thing.

Making the sails from terylene was another exercise that involved plans and careful measuring. Much as I enjoyed doing it, it was very different from the art of watercolour painting where sight, imagination and colour combine with the unknown and unpredicatable to produce a picture. As often as not, the end result comes as a surpirse, which may be a bitter disappointment or may be a great delight. Whether craft with its skilled and predictable familiarity appeals to you, or art with its skilled but less predictable quality draws you on, both are about creativity and both can be part of the spiritual journey.

Somewhere across the wide range of arts and crafts that we are now going to look at, from art as we traditionally understand it, on through creativity round the house and garden to making music and writing poetry, there should be something that fires your imagination.

■ I. COLOUR, COLLAGE AND CLAY

Let us not make life harder than necessary by beginning with a difficult medium like watercolour, though it has a delicacy and sensitivity worth exploring later on.

• How about being adventurous with **powder colour** on a large scale? I have had fun with large off-cuts of hardboard or chipboard by first coating them liberally with ordinary white emulsion left over from decorating; while still wet, I have added powder colours, stroking them into the fluid emulsion. The next stage is to use string, dead leaves, straw, sawdust or whatever is around to add to the picture using

more emulsion to stick them on and more powder to add colour to a design that can just happen. The floor may be about the only place to do this, using a large piece of plastic to protect the surface.

It is largely about the sort of imaginative play that just lets things happen. That goes for almost everything that follows.

• **Pastels** are convenient and easy to use and can be very delicate, though bold colours and designs might make a better exploratory beginning. Charcoal is similar and in my view is at its best on white paper; both may be 'fixed' with a spray fixative to prevent smudging once complete.

• **Pen drawing** is a good discipline if you like that sort of thing; there is no rubbing out of mistakes! My art teacher made me use a pen to learn to get it right first time. It is of course about learning to see what is there. Waterproof drawing pens can allow colour to be added; the non-waterproof ones do enable some interesting shading to be done with a wet brush, where the ink is deliberately encouraged to run.

• **Pencil drawing**. The common HB pencil together with a cartridge paper pad for outside sketching must be one of the most user friendly of art forms. The point can be soft or sharp, and

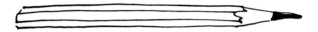

the lines thick or thin; a rubber can deal rapidly with mistakes without leaving a trace. Watercolour pencils are becoming increasingly popular and can be used simply as crayons, or can be stroked with a wet brush to get different effects.

• **Oil and acrylic** are easier to use than watercolour and are much more predictable and obedient, but do seem to have a lot of luggage attached to them. Both can use primed hardboard, chipboard, or specially prepared boards in place of expensive canvas. Acrylic is very versatile and being water based, does not have the persistent smell of oil. Providing you ensure that the paint does not dry out in the tubes and on the brushes, you will find it an excellent medium to experiment with.

• **Collage** and its close relatives, **montage** and **banner making**, can be explored by a group or done individually, which is true of most of the media we are looking at here. They can also open some quite fascinating ways of working with the Bible.

At its most basic, collage involves sticking bits and pieces to a surface, and those raw materials can be drawn from anywhere. PVA adhesive is good and so is UHU, though heavy things may need to be held more firmly with other fixings.

Montage includes using materials like newspaper cuttings and pictures, all stuck on to a surface to form a whole, while banner making is a major growth industry in churches up and down the land. Imaginative and beautiful homemade banners are appearing on walls to

focus some of the great themes of our faith. In some ways they are a reminder of the days before people could read and there was a much deeper reliance on visual imagery to express and communicate worship and belief. It is a timely reminder, because we need to use our eyes and imagination as much as we need to use our ears and our intellect. One of its virtues is that while it can be done at a highly skilled and complex level, it is perfectly possible to do it simply and effectively without prior skill. Shapes and letters cut out of felt can be stuck on in a vivid simple design that uses a wide range of fabrics of differing colours and textures.

A friend of mine, who makes banners at a highly profesional level, uses richly coloured lengths of corduroy as the backing and sticks on quite heavy fabrics and braids with adhesive; the impact is impressive. It is important to be simple and direct, and desirable not to fill the whole of the available space – so avoid trying to say everything in one banner.

As an all-age activity, banner making takes some beating; recently a group of us from children to grandparents spent part of a Sunday doing the Exodus story in this way. The backing was an old candlewick bedspread and the resources included dressmaking remnants and seeds; it was a splendid occasion, enjoyable and full of deep meaning.

• **Modelling clay** has to be experienced to be believed. There can be few materials more able to express feelings both in the process of actually using the clay and in the product at the end. At a workshop, a priest who had been pastorally involved in a number of suicides in recent

weeks used his clay to work through some of his
pain by modelling a face twisted with silent
grief. It was so powerful that at first the group
found it extremely difficult to handle such an
expression of anguish.

Whether clay is being used in a healing,
prayerful way like that, or whether in an
altogether more playful and light hearted
manner, it is versatile, easy to use and
enormously satisfying. It is a most basic art form
using earth, water and human hands, together
with the fire of imagination. The problem may
be in getting hold of it; craft shops may have
some, and obviously potteries carry a stock and

they might be willing to part with a bag. Play group suppliers sometimes have a branded product derived from clay containing a setting additive and nylon fibre to help the bonding. This dries hard without firing, is obviously convenient, but costs rather more than the real thing.

There is in fact no need to fire models initially, though you would no doubt aim for that eventually by joining a pottery group; but assuming you are going to begin on your own and have acquired some clay, use a lump about as big as two fists, together with a board to work on and a beaker of water for moistening fingers and wetting the material. It can be pleasantly messy, so use a protective sheet of newspaper or plastic. The primary tools are your own hands, but all sorts of things like pencils, nail files, bits of wood or hard plastic, can be pressed into service for shaping and marking. Start by playing with it, squeezing and moulding it, even throwing it down hard on your board a few times which is a splendid way of getting rid of some of that surplus aggression! Then let it lead you on to try figures and animals or abstract shapes that point towards the inexpressible. Give yourself freedom and let it happen.

■ 2. HOME AND GARDEN

It is the place where we spend a lot of time and probably it is where we are most truly ourselves. The barriers and defences are down and we are not under pressure to pretend. Here we eat and play, love, argue and relax, work and sleep. It is important to us beyond description and from an early age we can feel desperately home-sick if

we have to go away. Ideally it is a place of absolute security and safety, and we return to it with pleasure and relief whatever faults we know it inevitably has.

A place of such significance invites from us the best that we can do or be. Without really thinking that much about it, we are using creativity all the time in and around our houses, but let us look more closely and explore possibilities for being even more imaginative in our approach to flowers and food, to lighting and colour as well as to general D.I.Y. maintenance and gardening.

• **Flower arranging** has some very precise rules about what and what not to do. At the risk of causing some offence I would like to suggest that rules can get in the way of spontaneity in this as in all art forms. It was late Spring in the Forest of Dean where I was involved in a camping holiday for the families of men in prison; Debbie, a delightful little girl from our group brought me a bunch of bluebells and leaves that she had picked in the woods. A jam jar was all we had to put them in and they looked and felt perfect. On my kitchen table there is a small vase holding some dry grass, some brilliant red rose hips, the seed head of a rush and some greenery pulled from a stream. It was brought in by a visitor who had gone on an early morning walk before breakfast; the arrangement is uncontrived with no conscious thought of rules yet it has a graceful simplicity that catches the eye immediately.

I am not rubbishing the rules of flower arranging any more than I would rubbish the rules of perspective for drawing a building; what I am saying is that these things come after the spontaneity not before it. Sadly, the rules can sometimes rob that natural quality of its simple directness. There can be a sort of 'perfection' that keeps all the rules but is dead. I believe we need to learn to trust the intuition of the artist within us about what is right and about which colours belong naturally together. Such explorations take on excitement and challenge as different flowers are tried in different pots or vases with greenery or dried grass or a slender piece of broken branch and trailing ivy.

Some general guidelines would suggest that

you avoid overcrowding; a few flowers in a green setting can be more delicate than a mass of colour without any relief for the eye. Odd numbers of flowers feel more right than an even number, I am told, and I find that to be true for me. Our choice of flowers does not inevitably mean a costly trip to a florist either; there is something to be said for using the flowers that are in season where possible. My own preference is for the wild flowers of the countryside, where hedges are full of interest even in winter. The colours are more muted then, and the emphasis will not be on flowers as such, but there is still plenty to go at. Cities have their green and colourful places and not all such city places are forbidden territory to the sensitive seeker of flowers.

Before we leave this subject, we need to recall that some aggressive measures to control weeds and encourage plant growth have placed many species at risk, if not destroyed them altogether. Let us pick with reverence and care recognising that spirituality and ecological sensitivity belong together.

• **Food**. It would hardly be tactful to remind someone struggling to survive in the kitchen, with hungry mouths to feed and endless work to be done, that this is the time and place for a creative approach to food preparation.

Nonetheless, the gathering, preparation and sharing of food, must be one of the most basic of human functions relating to survival itself and to our social structures. At that social level, it can take on a powerfully ritual quality also. In the early days of my ministry in Lancashire, I was overwhelmed by the inevitable and unavoidable meal that followed every funeral. The poorest of mourners would never omit it for this was where family and friends met to talk and cry and often to laugh as well. It was an essential part of the grieving process.

At another level there can be few greater and simpler pleasures than sharing a meal with close friends. We pay great attention to that meal, not because we wish to impress or compete but because we care and somehow eating food together expresses that caring and love. The Lifestyle Movement has given us a profound insight into hospitality with the words: "Living

simply that others might simply live." Shared meals can reflect that insight; food does not have to be the most expensive, with the occasion becoming a costly and impressive display of wealth. Indeed such a display in a world where millions live at the edge of survival has an obscene quality. Attention to the beauty inherent in simple food does not cost money, but it does cost time, thoughtfulness and imagination. There are many natural colours and textures to explore. Imagine not having the brilliant colour of the humble tomato or the intertwining rings of onion or not having richly textured parsley to decorate the cheese. Salads have unlimited possibilities for an innovative approach, and what about home made bread and home grown herbs?

Before we leave food and on a sadly serious note, we have to ask some questions about factory farming methods. We note that part of our spirituality is to exercise responsibility for the earth and its creatures, and that involves thinking about how the meat we eat was produced and what the conditions were like where the eggs came from. Food in its production and distribution touches some very sensitive areas that we dare not ignore. Let us be mindful of that in our generous but simple hospitality.

•The manner in which **lighting** is used can make or destroy atmosphere. Most of us are romantic enough to like candles, but think how their unique quality is lost if the glaring overhead light is left on. Perhaps some people are simply not aware of these things or are untouched by them; maybe they think that colour does not interest them or affect how they feel in a room. I believe that we are touched by these qualities whether we are aware of them or not, which is why lighting does matter.

Imagination in this direction need not cost a lot of money. Inexpensive table lamps do the same job as exotic costly ones and their very simplicity may well be part of their attractiveness. Pretentious fittings can soon go over the top and appear almost vulgar. Table lamps, carefully placed, can work wonders for the most unexciting of rooms and conversely one single overhead centrally placed light can ruin a potentially beautiful space. If the light is harshly bright, it might well be functional but hurts the eyes and hardens all the edges; if it is dull it gives the place a heavy and unwelcoming quality. Pools of gentle light give warmth and intimacy, and that candlelit meal with a few friends, sharing simple basic food prepared sensitively and beautifully and using materials that were produced without cruelty, can be a very special occasion.

Part of the task of this book is to draw attention to the rich and limitless possibilities there are at every turn for us to have beauty and order in our lives. There is enough gruesome ugliness about, without us making life worse by ignoring what could be full of wonder.

• Homes, more than anywhere, need to be places of beauty and order – not a stuffy or precious overdone sort of order, but a natural and harmonious way of being home.
Maintaining the house and garden can often seem to be hard and unfinishable work, but it is all part of the same overall strategy.

Should you ever suggest that there is work to

be done on the house, that suggestion is hardly likely to galvanise the family into action with paintbrushes and Polyfilla. Neither is it very likely that we shall spend time in our church study groups looking at spirituality and wallpapering. Gardening might just get a mention on this one, since gardens and God have more readily had a natural affinity. D.I.Y. and house maintenance belong much more to duty and necessity than to soulfulness and prayer. But if your liberated artist is given a free hand and a few guidelines around the house, what might there be in store?

The farmhouse and buildings where we live were gently falling into disrepair when we bought the place at an auction some years ago. There were no drains and the water main came to the back door and went no further. Windows were rotten and there was hardly a roof that did not leak and the garden had the delightful character of a partly cultivated wild life park.

Surrounded as we were by this chaos, other work still had to go on which was primarily counselling, running workshops and growing food. In between professional commitments

renovations began and continued; each summer since arriving here we have taken five or six weeks off to concentrate on major building work and this has also served to give a break from an emotionally demanding ministry. This has meant, for instance, putting up scaffolding in order to strip sections of roof, replace rotten timber, put on new felt and then replace the tiles. It has involved a lot of learning, and over the years it has been a creative experience and a therapeutic one. Sometimes there was acute anxiety at the sheer enormity of a job, and sometimes there was tiredness and despair, but always at the end there was a deep sense of satisfaction and purpose.

Gradually the place began to come alive as wood and stone, concrete, PVC and steel, colours, materials and textures were handled thoughfully and tentatively and always with hope.

It was work, but more than that. It was pleasure, but more than that also. It was creativity but even that word is insufficient. It was and is part of a spiritual journey in the presence of God handling the raw materials of creation itself. And not only the raw materials of the earth, for there is history in these stones where people were born; they lived, worked, loved, played and died here.

Everywhere we go in this world and whatever we do, we are in the loving presence of God and in living history; therefore we should tread with sensitivity and care even as we prepare a wall for papering or dig soil for our beans and flowers. 'The earth is God's and all that is in it.' In the end it comes down to the values we live by and the attitudes we have to what we are doing. Jesus reminds us that whatever we do to one of the least, we are doing to Him.

Staying with D.I.Y. and the creative spiritual journey, what about **plumbing**? Water and pipes, taps and drains would hardly be the first candidates for inclusion in thoughts about spiritual exercises or art forms. But struggling with routes and bends for pipes, tanks and their fittings is certainly perplexing and ultimately creative. The amazing sense of exhilaration when the stoptap is finally opened and the water flows without leaks is a wonderful experience. God loves pleasure. The heartwarming delight of the amateur plumber when the water finally flows is as pleasing to God as the glorious singing of Sunday's congregation!

I fully realise that the thought of putting in some pipes or decorating a wall may not quicken the pulse with anticipation, and yet the practical impact on the household is enormous when colours are changed, or things work that previously did not. When the liberated artist gets unlocked with woodchip paper and colour, seed catalogues and what have you, things happen and God sees that it is good.

• **Gardening**. Let us not get into romantic unreality about the soil because it is hard work, though immensely rewarding. It is sufficient to grow things just because they are beautiful and it is good to grow things healthily for food. We use companion planting where possible, and that means having a riot of French marigolds alongside the carrots, and it really does keep the destructive carrotfly away. Organic gardening is essentially more creative than using pesticides and weedkillers which we know in our hearts not to be the best way. What is ecologically unacceptable is unacceptable to God. Destructive treatment of the earth is ultimately a destruction of our own lives and therefore a denial of true spirituality.

Gardeners who let their artist out love riots of splendid colour and they love shadowed mysterious places. Has your garden got some hidden unused corner that could have its mystery developed with small shrubs and flowers and perhaps a seat? Growing all manner of plants from cuttings is quite absorbing, and financially worthwhile. And what about water? Small ponds are easy enough to make, though garden centres sell PVC or fibre glass units ready to pop into a hole. If you want to make your own, you need some heavy grade PVC as a waterproof layer and some old pieces of carpet to protect the membrane from being pierced by stones. Having dug your hole, first put in some old carpet then the PVC membrane followed by some more carpet; then add some soil for plants to grow in. Around the edge you might care to arrange some large stones which look attractive and also hold down the edges. A visit to the local garden centre will give more ideas about the sort of plants that flourish in and around water. Birds, butterflies and a host of wild things will love your pond and there will always be something interesting happening around water.

Should you have no outside space and therefore no garden the limits are obvious. However, indoor plants, which can be simple or quite exotic, are readily available, but they do need a lot of attention and care. A house I was in recently has a variegated ivy growing up the dining room wall and literally clinging to it. Apparently it needs a vigorous trim from time to time to check its tendency to take over the whole place. Window boxes and hanging baskets can add rich and interesting colours in otherwise dull and unlikely places. Small varieties of fuschia are particularly good and keep flowering for a long time.

■ 3. UNUSUAL WAYS OF BEING CREATIVE

This is the point where we really get serious about a green approach to art! It begins with what is thrown away and there is plenty to go at. One day I will do what I have wanted to do for years with scrap from an old car; the engine block and contents of the gear box fascinate me. I want to use my welding equipment to create something from those heavy chunky pieces of metal. Initially it would not have to mean anything at a profoundly significant level as a sort of social or political statement; it is sufficient for it to be enjoyable. Having said that, I suspect that in the end it would come to mean something that is very profound. Some of the shapes, textures and machined surfaces of parts of a car engine can be strikingly beautiful, and to create a unified whole out of those scrap pieces, to clean it down and paint it matt black or grey, could produce a starkly powerful work of art; the fascinating shapes are what they are and need no justifiation. There must be a whole lot of things in God's creation which are not strictly essential to the physical balance of the environment; they are there because they are. It is enough to have the longing to create.

You may not wish to begin with welding equipment and scrap cars but waste is everywhere and although words like 'art' and 'waste' are not immediately linked in our consciousness, the artist that you let out does and will link them. It is also a timely parable that infinite possibilities reside in rubbish bins, scrap yards and waste tips. Almost anything from the waste bin that is clean and dry will do; PVA adhesive will stick a wide range of materials together while nails and screws can handle the heavy work. It can be two or three dimensional, and may hang, move or sit still. Resources include wood, paper, card, polystyrene packaging, string, tins, lids and fabrics to name but a few, and along with the waste, more conventional art materials can be used to add colour and texture.

Start by playing or doodling with bits and pieces if no immediate task presents itself. Once you begin, random ideas emerge and flow as shapes, textures and colours relate and harmonise. Interestingly, the mind begins to reflect at the same time as all sorts of ideas float to the surface which are worth attending to or noting for later. Never underestimate the dynamic nature of thoughtful reflection while you are being artistic. Play it may be, but play is serious business.

• **Wood**. As a child growing up on a farm in Hampshire, I was captivated by the mystery of trees and fell in love with woods and wood. I well remember an old countryman teaching me how to cut a young sapling from the hedge to make a whistle that would play tunes. Willow and ash were the best, though horse chestnut was almost as good. He also taught me to whittle the wood which meant decorating the instrument by cutting into the bark and trimming the ends, and being a very religious child, I soon learned to play hymns on my whistle! In these days of environmental awareness, we had better not cut into young trees for our supplies, and instead can content ourselves with offcuts, driftwood or old left over pieces from discarded furniture. All of these can already have the beginnings of something special even before we work on them. There is no need to have a wide range of sophisticated tools when first playing with wood; initially a sharp blade, a saw and some sandpaper will go a long way. If it feels good and right, and that it is something you want to pursue, then a wide range of basic tools is readily available. My father in his seventies went on to acquire a small lathe and began to design and make things like table lanps and egg cups for his grandchildren. It had a simple beginning and went on for another ten years.

David Moore, a friend of mine now living in Bradford, does fascinating things with wood destined for the fire; he sees all sorts of possibilities in the most unlikely pieces. When he was last here he went through the woodshed and took away a selection that he has now worked into shapes that are both mysterious and beautiful; some are abstract and others are more representational. Roots from the elder tree have strange twisted shapes and so does ivy that has grown old round the branch of a dead tree. Some pieces look almost human and strangely full of feeling even before you begin. Driftwood can be similarly evocative where it has been battered by rocks and waves and smoothed by sand. A further cut here or there, and a little shaping and there is a work of art. Be gentle with the wood and do not force it; follow the grain and go with it and let it become what it will be. Listen and be attentive to it and be

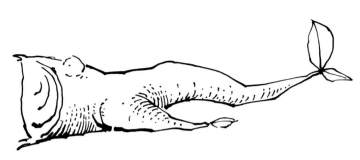

humble before it, for you are handling the
things of God. A coat of matt varnish will bring
out the delicate beauty of the grain, and the
final move might be to mount it on a simple
stand and give it a name. Things like to have
their own names.

■ 4. POETRY AND MUSIC

Sarah is nervously standing out there in front of
the congregation, the paper shaking in her
hands. She has never been up front before.
Then she begins to read her own words, her
own poetry – something she said the day before
she had never done, and never could do. But
she did, and we were moved deeply to hear it.
Perhaps our ideas of what constitutes a poem
make it impossible for us to try writing one.

Maybe we feel it ought to rhyme or ought to have four lined verses, or should sound like a hymn.

In workshops, I try to remove all those expectations and invite people to write what they feel, and to do it in very short lines down the paper, using as few words as possible. 'But I can't do that,' Margaret said at a workshop in Whitby. My reply was to suggest that she make that statement the first line of her poem, and then move on from there by going back to the Biblical text we had been using, and by looking out of the window in order to see the sea and the sky and by responding with simple direct language. She did precisely that, and her words were a true inspiration. I am frequently surprised and impressed by the feelingful, direct and powerful writing that people do with no prior experience. It does however require a stimulus; it is not possible I think, just to sit down and write poetry at will. It generally comes out of deep pain or intense joy; the expression of that pain or joy in some appropriate way is necessary for our good health, and writing poetry is one of those very appropriate ways.

I am forced to recognise that most of the poetry I have heard in numerous workshops

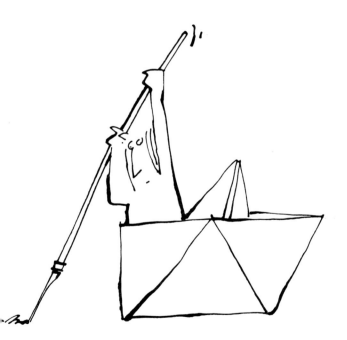

over the years is sad. My conclusion is that this sadness and pain is waiting in there to be acknowledged, expressed and healthily released. Like working with clay, it can be a profoundly healingful experience. I would always suggest that if you are writing from the depths of your heart, that you find someone you trust in order to share with them what you are saying.

• **Making music** is another dimension that might be your world as you set your artist free; if you already play an instrument you could be part way there. Let us recall that before the days of printing there was little available in the way of manuscript music, and no doubt many ordinary people in towns and villages learned to play tunes by ear, and developed those tunes with infinite variations. We would not be without the immeasurable musical enrichment brought by our cassette or CD players, but their negative impact on creativity in music must be enormous. So how about going back in time a bit, and playing around with your instrument using familiar words but creating your own melody? Take a verse that means a lot to you, preferably something short and direct and work out a theme. Leave harmonies out of it for the time being. I did something last month while travelling to an appointment, humming it and singing it in the car. The words came from my prayers that morning and were:

"Send forth your light and truth; let these be my guide."

You might care to do something similar with words that are important for you, and you could then incorporate them in your prayers, singing them over and over as the verse goes deeper and deeper into your soul.

It would be quite impossible to prepare a comprehensive list of areas where our creativity might be set free to enrich our spirituality and feed into the whole of our lives, but before we move on, let us briefly look at just one or two more. At a Retreat for clergy in Yorkshire, the participants each had opportunity to share with the group some special interest. The one I remember best was David's calligraphy. His intense excitement and enthusiasm for it was magnetic. It is not an easy thing to do, but there is real delight in that careful patient working of words and design. I sometimes suggest that poets write out some of their special poetry in this way.

• How is your **camera**? How about trying pictures from unusual angles or from inside a building looking out? Freda used up a whole roll of film here one day simply wandering round the farm buildings, inside and out, taking pictures by looking through doorways, or from inside looking out, or through a window with broken glass, and past spiders' webs and a whole range of shots through stacked timber and rubbish. I have never seen such imaginative photography in one set of exposures.

• **Computer graphics** have arrived more recently on the scene, and if you have access to the equipment, then the most up-to-the-minute technology becomes yet another tool in your creative hands. At the other extreme and to end the list, traditional basket making, with all the infinite variations of colour and texture in the

willow, can be worked to your own designs.
They make excellent presents too.

■ EXERCISE 6

The AIM is to reflect on the suggestions and
make some important choices.

• Look back over the suggestions and note the
ones that caught your imagination and stirred
your interest.

• Did you say 'I will' or 'I can't'? and what are
you going to do about it?

• Make a list of the ones you are interested in,
and note the materials you will need.

• Decide on which you will try first, and decide
when you are going to start. Think about
whether it might be helpful to make an informal
contract with someone to help you keep to your
commitment. The encouragement of another
goes a very long way.

6

CREATIVITY GROUPS

ANOTHER SORT OF Pandora's Box that can be opened with powerful consequences is the experience of working in a group. When the group meets specifically to use creativity as a way of doing theology or Bible study or as a worship resource, surprising doors are opened and people learn a lot about themselves. In that sense there is a healing dimension to it also. In groups where I am involved there is a meditative emphasis with times of stillness and we almost always use biblical material, though there are many other sources that could be used. The profoundly spiritual creativity that happens in those settings is deeply prayerful and therapeutic. There are some useful ground rules that assist the group to get into the process and to get more out of it.

1. Skill is not necessary.
2. There is no competition or judging.
3. Silence during creative time is extremely

desirable where appropriate.

4. Space should be made available towards the end, for participants to share and talk together about the experience.

A possible pattern for a meditative creativity workshop that lasts one and half to two hours is the following and it is in three distinct parts.

■ PART 1. INDUCTION

This is the time to put people at their ease about the method, about resource materials and time-tabling. The list of ground rules above would be helpful at this point.

I normally use some simple relaxation exercises also, as part of the preparation, sometimes right at the beginning.

The actual theme for the workshop is the last thing I introduce before people begin creating.

■ PART 2. CREATION

Participants need to be comfortable with their own choice of materials – the simplest are powder paint, pastels, clay and writing things, but more ambitious possibilities could develop.

In the quietness, they explore, play and experiment as ideas and images begin to surface.

30-45 minutes are needed for this, though an experienced group might want much longer.

■ PART 3. REFLECTION

The group is called back together and if they agree, the work is put on the floor in the middle of the circle – I usually use a candle as a focus. At this point the leader sensitively invites comment and conversation, though no one should ever be pushed into talking. The group is encouraged but never compelled to share freely.

Some groups like to bring the event to an end with more quiet and perhaps some singing of Taizé chants, choruses or hymns. Where Holy Communion is the norm of the church involved, a creative Eucharist drawing on the above pattern can be a rich and beautiful time with a high degree of participation. Prayers of intercession done by painting and thanksgivings modelled in clay, with penitence expressed through poetry, can take the group into something quite unique. My experience of such

Eucharists over the years is that they need every bit of two hours, and more if possible. This is particularly so where the event is a residential one. Levels of involvement and commitment are so high that only good things can happen as people of all ages combine to create simple drama while others are working at dance. Everyone does their best, and everything is accepted; the emphasis is not on being perfect but on being involved.

■ EXERCISE 7

The AIM is to explore your experience of groups, determining what was helpful and what was not.

Recall memories of occasions in groups inside the church and out, at home and at conferences.

What made you feel comfortable, safe and relaxed and enabled you to participate?

What disturbed and threatened you and inhibited your sharing?

Write about those feelings and focus hard and thoughtfully on what the enabling qualities were. How would you feel about gathering a small group together to do something creative?

What would your hopes and fears be for such an exercise?

Listen carefully to your own hopes and fears, write about them, question their validity and affirm the good things. Share your thoughts with your friend.

When you are thinking about holidays or retreats, you might care to get information from the following organisations about ecumenical events that link a wide range of creative activities with the spiritual journey. Stamped addressed envelopes might be appreciated.

- **The National Retreat Centre,** Liddon House, 24 Audley Street, London W1Y 5DL. They publish an annual journal called *Vision* with lots of information in.
- **Theme Retreats,** Canon Charles Shells, 13 Dod Lane, Glastonbury, Somerset BA6 8BZ
- **Methodist Guild Holidays,** Derwent House, Cromford, Matlock, Derbyshire DE4 5JG

■ 7

WHEN THE RIVER RUNS DRY

FINALLY, WE NEED to look at what happens when nothing happens. It is painful and can be fiercely destructive having tried so hard only to find nothing – or so it seems. The wilderness does not seem to be a good place when it is deep inside the human soul; it is hard when inspiration stops and possibly harder still if it seems never to have happened at all. So what are we to do with this ugly thing we call 'failure'? Thinking about the exciting possibilities of creativity would be unrealistic if we did not also look at its shadow side, where the fear of failure waits to destroy us. It may take some time to uncover our gifts and that is threatening in itself; it can so easily lead to the conviction often expressed, that we have no creative artistic gifts anyway. That is simply not true. It does require courage to go on with the search, but go on with it we must, for it is worth it in the end. We need to try different ways and different settings and working alongside and with different people. An evening class for beginners in the area of your choice could well open a door. One of the keys to creativity is the liberated imagination that sees new possibilities in the most unlikely places. Courage puts the inspiration to work and makes the dream a practical reality. Occupational Therapists working in clinics and hospitals know well enough the healing power of creativity as demoralised victims of crippling accidents or illnesses start to live again. They rediscover meaning and purpose as they tentatively begin to use their hands to make simple things. It is that first beginning that matters, and once started the process has a momentum of its own.

'Don't just stand there; do something!' might not be the most perceptive and gentle of commands, but it is an idea. Get that large piece of hardboard and paint it with white emulsion and get some powder paint or acrylic on to it, then spread seeds or sawdust here and there. Now stick some dead leaves on to the wet paint in an uncomplicated pattern. Keep it simple and leave plenty of space.

It might be good to get a group together willing to play with paint and willing to do something as a joint effort in the following not too serious way. Stick several pieces of paper together with tape to make a large square and have a supply of pastels or powder paint so that each participant can get at them. Then invite the group to start drawing or painting without any further conversation. Stop when the paper is full and talk about the experience. It could be a way of getting past a block.

It is hard to handle a dry time that follows a productive spell; the sense of disappointment and even anger can be bitter. I had a long and bleak break from painting beginning in my mid-twenties and lasting for a decade. In that time I tried so many ways to recover the lost delight of previous years when art had been awakened in me by an attentive and caring teacher. I tried without success and sadly came to believe I would paint no more. But quite suddenly it all started again and the stimulus was to do some pen and wash paintings to help raise money for our Church in Glazebury. Apart from some occasional spells since then, watercolour painting has always been around. From time to time it does threaten to dry up and that reminds me that we are for ever at the edge of failure and success with a narrow dividing line between. It is at this point of weakness that a true strength emerges; there is a true humility in the sense of wonder that the good thing ever happens at all. We do not control our creativity for it is a gift that we can only accept at the moment it is given.

• **Being**. It is hard to be still and to wait, but we need to learn the art; I believe it is good to find a place, a real place to go to where we can be truly still, and to go there often. If that place of stillness evades us, is it possible to create something at home by using a candle to focus our attentiveness? In the quiet we ask what the wilderness is saying. If we can see it, the experience when the river runs dry is prime learning and growing time; this is where we wait and listen. It is part of our own inner rhythm like the seasons; waves of intense productivity are followed by what appears to be sterility. If we can keep hold of the truth that

we are channels of God's creating, the awareness of that is never so profound as when failure and darkness are threatening.

• **Doing**. The other side of relaxed inner stillness is about getting out walking and doing and taking in all that we can. Whatever the weather, get into it with all senses tuned to receive, not only seeing but touching and hearing, tasting and smelling. In our densely civilised and highly sophisticated culture we can so easily lose touch with the movement of the seasons and the sacramental quality of the cosmos and its createdness. We nurture that insight by getting mud on our shoes and wind and rain in our hair, as well as by enjoying September's soft warm sun and 'mellow fruitfulness'. When the springs of creativity well up again, they will not be unconnected with the vulnerable stillness of being and the sensitive openness of doing.

• **Writing**. Some people keep journals as a way of reflecting on what is happening; it is good to write about your creativity, especially when it is in recession. The act of writing somehow clears the air and helps recover

balance and perspective; it combines both the being and the doing for it involves quiet thoughtfulness with positive active writing. In the same way that creativity can be prayer, so can writing. In the accepting quiet of it, it will be possible to sense the gentlest movement of the breath of God, for every moment is 'In the beginning.'

■ EXERCISE 8

The AIM is to reflect on times of dryness with the intention of learning all that is possible from the experience.

This is very much an exercise to work through with someone else you like and trust.

Look back over the years and note down some of the times of dryness. What did you feel? What or who enabled you to come out of that place?

Look back to occasions of blossoming creativity and note how they felt. What do you imagine enabled them to happen?

Write a letter to yourself, accepting and understanding your feelings, challenging the negative thoughts and pointing out the helpful truths you need to affirm.

Read that letter to yourself again and again for it is a prayer that God hears.

■ ENDPIECE

YOU HAVE LET your artist out and found
some of your deep creativity; it may well
have taken much courage and struggle along
with the pleasure. I hope that you found it was
not quite so impossible as you had at first
imagined. I hope too that you have had and will
continue to have the warm feeling of approving
friends who said with some disbelief 'did you do
that all on your own?'!

Did you try carving some drift wood or was it
clay that you stroked and pressed into shape?
Perhaps it was a small pond in your garden that
you made and now the birds and flowers are all
around it. Was it a banner for Easter or a
tapestry which you are going to make to your
own design next time? What about groups? Did
you get a small number of people together to do
some painting? Whatever it was, you took the
decision and you followed it through. The
hardest part was that decision to get started and
to get past the blocks and barriers.

Maybe the most profound truth of all is that

creativity is not ours alone. It comes welling up from the depths of the Holy One before time began, pouring its beautiful colours and textures and its mystical poetry and music in a great flood of haunting passionate mystery that celebrates love across the world. The simple and amazing truth is that God delights in creativity.